MR. MEN AND *little Miss*

ANNUAL 1999

D1461778

Original concept by Roger Hargreaves
New text by John Malam
Illustrated by Adam and Giles Hargreaves
Designed by Maggie Aldred

MR. MEN   LITTLE MISS

£5.50
UK ONLY

MR. MEN AND *Little Miss*

ANNUAL 1999

"You will find your favourite Mr Men and Little Miss friends on these pages..."

Contents

Mr Nosey
I'm on page 24

Mr Muddle
I'm on pages
24 and 36

Little Miss Tiny
I'm on page 26

Mr Snow
I'm on page 28

Mr Cheerful
I'm on page 29

Mr Rush
I'm on
page 30

Mr Sneeze
I'm on
page 32

Little Miss Shy
I'm on page 38

Mr Forgetful
I'm on page 44

Little Miss
Contrary
I'm on
page 42

Little Miss Star
I'm on page 47

Little Miss
Scatterbrain
I'm on
page 48

Mr Tall
I'm on
page 40

Little Miss Late
I'm on page 45

Little Miss Brainy
I'm on page 50

Little Miss Magic
I'm on
page 56

Mr Bump
I'm on page 58

Mr Small
I'm on page 51

Mr Happy

Mr Happy lives in Happyland. He couldn't possibly live anywhere else, could he? For instance, you wouldn't find him living in a place called Unhappyland, would you? Mr Happy only wants to live in the happiest land there is, with lots of other happy, smiling people.

In Happyland everyone smiles and feels happy all day long. Even the cats and dogs, worms and snails, birds and bees are happy in Happyland. And the flowers. And even the weeds. And the trees, too. In fact, the trees feel so happy that they grow higher... and higher... and higher... until you can't see the tops of them. They must be at least one hundred feet tall!

There's something else special about Happyland, too. The sun shines all day long. It only rains at night, when Mr Happy is tucked

in Happyland

up, fast asleep in his bed.

Lucky Mr Happy! He can play outside all day every day because the weather is always bright and sunny – just like he is! No wonder he's such a happy person!

Mr Happy lives in a little cottage by a lovely lake. He wakes up early every morning, and the first thing he does is pull back his bedroom curtains and look out of the window.

He looks across to the mountains on the other side of the lake. As the sun comes up from behind them, Mr Happy's smile turns up at the corners of his mouth and grows bigger... and bigger... and bigger. It's the best start to a happy new day in Happyland!

Now, one morning, not long ago, something very unusual happened.

Mr Happy was waiting for the sun to start shining. He waited. And carried on waiting. His smile began to crinkle up on his lips.

7

"Mmm," and then: "Well, I never!"

High above the hundred-foot-tall trees, and above the tips of the tallest mountains, in the very place where the sun should have been, there was a fluffy white cloud. And coming out of the cloud was the brightest, the most colourful, the biggest rainbow you could ever imagine.

Mr Happy opened his eyes as wide as saucers, and his smile stretched from ear to ear. He'd never seen a rainbow in Happyland before.

Now you might think that it's impossible to catch a rainbow. And that's

He started to look a little bit unhappy. "This is very strange," he said. "I'll go and see what's happening."

Outside, on the shore at the edge of the lake, a crowd of cats and dogs, worms and snails, birds and bees had gathered. They were looking at something in the sky.

Mr Happy looked, too. "Oh," he said, quickly followed by:

perfectly true of course, but as you know, Happyland is where the happiest of things can happen. So, when Mr Happy cupped his hands together and held them out, it didn't surprise him that the rainbow simply jumped into them!

Mr Happy began to walk away from the lake, back up the winding path to his cottage. He walked very carefully, and quite slowly, taking great care not to let go of the rainbow.

Every few steps, Mr Happy stopped and looked over his shoulder. He saw that the fluffy cloud was moving too, and as it moved, Mr Happy saw something peeping out from behind it.

By the time Mr Happy reached his house, the rainbow had grown paler and paler until he wasn't sure if it was there at all.

He looked for the cloud, but that had vanished too, over the mountains and far away. And in its place, just where it should have been all along, was the early morning sun, shining warm and bright.

"Hurray!" said Mr Happy. "It's going to be another happy day in Happyland."

Can you read this?

A puzzle about Happyland

Mr Happy would like to ask you a question about Happyland, and when you've read the story on the previous two pages you'll know the answer straight away.

BUT CAN YOU READ THE QUESTION?

Mr Happy has written it in "mirror writing". To see it the right way round, try looking at it in a mirror.

How tall are the trees in Happyland?

I think the trees in Happyland are...

one thousand feet tall

one hundred feet tall

ten feet tall

10

Make a Mr Greedy mobile

1 Draw round the plate and saucer. Add Mr Greedy's legs. Cut him out.

2 Draw round the saucer. Draw a cake inside the circle. Cut out the circle and cake. Colour both sides of Mr Greedy and the cake.

3 Make small holes in the cake and in Mr Greedy's tummy. Loop a short length of cotton through. Tie a knot.

4 Make a hole in the top of Mr Greedy's head. Loop a longer piece of cotton through. Tie a knot. Draw Mr Greedy's face.

5 Draw Mr Greedy's fingers on his tummy. Hang your mobile up.

11

Little Miss Sunshine's
SEASONS

Did you know that Little Miss Sunshine can make even the most miserable person feel happy? For instance, when she visited the King of Miseryland she made him feel so sunny and cheerful that he decided to become the King of Laughterland! Now he feels like smiling all year round, from January to December, from Spring to Winter. Just see...

March • April • May

SPRING
in Laughterland

Birds make nests and raise their young. Daffodils, snowdrops and tulips open out. Leaves start to grow on trees. The King of Laughterland smiles because this is the time when lambs are born.

June • July • August

SUMMER
in Laughterland

Wheat and barley ripen in the fields. Trees are in full leaf. Swallows fly in from faraway lands. The King of Laughterland smiles because this is the time when butterflies can be seen.

Which season do you like the most?

AUTUMN
in Laughterland

Fruit, berries and nuts ripen. Leaves turn brown, yellow and red, and start to fall. The King of Laughterland smiles because this is the time when he sees squirrels hiding food for the winter.

WINTER
in Laughterland

Ponds are covered in ice. The trees are bare. Hedgehogs sleep through the winter in nests of leaves. The King of Laughterland smiles because this is the time when he plays in the snow.

Mr Funny's holiday postcards

1 Mr Funny drives a very funny car. It isn't an ordinary car at all. It doesn't have windows. It doesn't have a roof. Mr Funny's car is a shoe!

2 He likes to send a postcard from wherever he goes. In Tiddletown, Mr Nosey peeped over Mr Funny's shoulder as he wrote his postcard out!

3 In Nonsenseland, where grass is blue and trees are red, he met Little Miss Dotty. She gave him a sausage to write with instead of a pen!

4 In Sleepyland he called to see Mr Lazy. But he was fast asleep inside Yawn Cottage. Even the pillar box seemed sleepy. And the postman!

SSSCRAATCH!

5 In Twoland he saw Little Miss Twins. "Hello! Hello!" they said. Mr Funny pressed his car horn. BEEP! BEEP! it went. He posted two postcards.

6 In Loudland, where people SHOUT, Mr Quiet was reading. As Mr Funny wrote a postcard, his pen went SS-CRAA-TCH! "Sshh!" said Mr Quiet.

7 In Muddleland, Mr Funny asked Little Miss Contrary to choose a postcard for him. But she chose a birthday card instead. "Oops!" she said.

8 In Bigtown, Mr Funny's car had a puncture. Did Mr Uppity help mend it? He jolly well didn't! He wouldn't even tell him where to find a pillar box!

9 In Tiddlyville a crowd of people were waiting to see ever-so-famous Little Miss Star. She wrote her name on Mr Funny's postcard. He was so excited!

10 In Coldland Mr Funny caught a cold from Mr Sneeze. "ATISHOO!" they both said. Mr Funny shivered so much his writing went all shaky!

11 It was time for Mr Funny to go somewhere warm. He went to Sunnytown to visit Little Miss Fickle, from where he sent his last postcard.

12 Who do you think Mr Funny was sending postcards to? Well, when he got home he found lots of postcards on his mat. Now do you know?!

Mr Clever helps Mr Dizzy

Mr Clever likes to think he is the cleverest person in the whole world... and he probably is. He lives in Cleverland, where even the worms and the birds can read books.

Mr Dizzy lives in Cleverland, too. He's one of Mr Clever's not-so-clever friends. For instance, when Mr Clever asked Mr Dizzy what the opposite of "thin" was, he said "round". And when Mr Clever asked him what the opposite of "square" was, he said "fat". Mr Dizzy gets things all mixed up!

Mr Clever decided to help Mr Dizzy. You can help him too, by helping him to answer Mr Clever's five questions.

1 "Mr Dizzy, which is the odd worm out?"

2 "Mr Dizzy, which bird is the odd one out?"

3 "Mr Dizzy, which plate has five sweets on it?"

4 "Mr Dizzy, which flower has six petals?"

5 "Mr Dizzy, which balloon is Mr Small holding on to?"

How well did Mr Dizzy do? Check the answers on page 61.

Funny things happen in Nonsenseland!

Nonsenseland is a very funny place. **3** of the funniest people you will ever meet live there. There's [ ] , [ ] , and, of course, [ ] . In Nonsenseland the [ ] are as [ ] as [ ] jam, and the [ ] is as [ ] as the [ ] ! And that's not all that's funny in Nonsenseland. [ ] wear [ ] and [ ]s fly backwards! Have you ever heard of such a funny place? [ ] lives in a [ ] at the top of a [ ] ! He thinks it's the best place to be. He would, wouldn't he? He likes to eat [ ] on [ ] . YUK! And he sleeps in a [ ] , in his bedroom, in his funny little [ ] perched on top of his

Mr. Silly

little Miss Dotty

funny ! One day, when [Mr. Nonsense] opened his bedroom and looked out of his [window], he saw that everywhere was covered in a thick [rug] of [snow]. In Nonsenseland [snowflakes] are the colour of [bananas]. That's right – it snows [yellow] snow! [Mr. Nonsense] saw a [top hat] lying on top of the snow. He used his [comb] to telephone [Mrs. Clown]. (He wouldn't use an ordinary [telephone] would he?) "Bring a [spoon] to dig with," he said. But instead of a [spoon] she brought 2 old [cups]! "They will have to do," said [Mr. Nonsense]. They dug the snow away from around the [top hat]. And who should they find but [Mr. Nonsense]! He'd fallen asleep standing up, and the yellow [snowflakes] had covered him up from his [slippers] to his [top hat]! When he was uncovered, they made a yellow [snowman]. What fun in Nonsenseland!

Mr.Nonsense

Little Miss Greedy's

spot the difference

Little Miss Greedy is having a picnic outside Cherrycake Cottage. And what a picnic it is! Have you ever seen so many chocolate cakes, fruit cakes, cream cakes, and, of course, cherry cakes? Can you spot five things that are different in the bottom picture?

Check your answers on page 61.

Make a caterpillar with Mr Silly

Look on page 26 for some more creepy-crawlies!

YOU WILL NEED
cardboard egg boxes
paints
elastic
a darning needle

1 Divide the eggboxes into separate pieces.

2 Paint the pieces in bright colours. Leave to dry.

3 Paint eyes and a mouth on to one of the pieces.

4 Ask a grown-up to thread the needle with the elastic. Push it through each painted piece.

5 After the last piece has been threaded, tie a knot in the end of the elastic.

Fly the flag with Mr Tickle

Mr Tickle has been busy making flags for six of his friends. Can you decide which flag belongs to which friend? Look at each picture on each flag – who does the picture suit best?

1 Someone who likes cakes... lots and lots of them!

2 Someone who always asks "why?"

3 Someone who falls over a lot... OUCH!

Little Miss Magic

Mr. Bump

Mr. Noisy

Mr. Greedy

Little Miss Twins

In Twoland you will find two the same of everything. There are two red cars, two blue cars; two big boats, two little boats; two moons at night, and two suns in the day. This is where Little Miss Twin and Little Miss Twin live. They're identical in every way, like two peas in a pod, two birds in a bush, or two stars in the sky.

It's hard to tell the twins apart. Can you imagine how confusing that is?

Little Miss Greedy had a great time at the party. She would, wouldn't she? There were

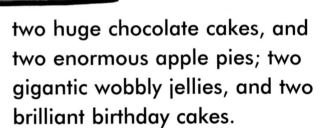

two huge chocolate cakes, and two enormous apple pies; two gigantic wobbly jellies, and two brilliant birthday cakes.

"Help yourself yourself," said the Little Miss Twins. (Isn't it funny how people who live in Twoland say the last word of a sentence twice?)

Little Miss Greedy didn't need to be asked twice. But not even she could manage to eat everything. She left two tiny crumbs on her plate. "I'm saving those for later," she said.

Then there were two loud knocks on the front door of Twotimes Cottage. KNOCK! KNOCK!

"Oh good good! Someone else has come to our party party!" the twins said together.

But when they opened the door,

in Twoland

Twoland

there was no one there. "That's funny funny," they said. "We're sure someone really did knock on the door door."

Then there were two more knocks, even louder than before. KNOCK!! KNOCK!!

The Little Miss Twins went to the back door. It looked exactly the same as the front door of Twotimes Cottage. Two letterboxes, two door handles... and two keyholes. And who should be peeping through both keyholes at the same time, but Mr Nosey.

"What's going on here?" he asked, nosily.

The Little Miss Twins invited him to come inside Twotimes Cottage... and that was the last they saw of him for the rest of the day.

Mr Nosey was so nosey he couldn't stop opening doors and drawers, books and boxes, and cupboards and cabinets. And because there were two of everything inside Twotimes Cottage, Mr Nosey quickly forgot what he'd looked inside, and what he hadn't! And so he started all over again... and then again... and again! You wouldn't expect him to do anything else would you?

Little Miss Tiny finds out

Little Miss Tiny lives in a very unusual place. She lives in a mousehole. A mouse nibbled it right through the dining-room skirting board at Home Farm. When the mouse moved out, Little Miss Tiny moved in... and so did some creepy-crawlies.

EARWIG
about 20 millimetres long

An earwig has wings, but it hardly ever uses them. It keeps them folded neatly away on its back. Little Miss Tiny has never seen an earwig fly – but she has seen one run and climb very quickly. An earwig has two pincers at the end of its body. They look like tweezers. When it is in danger it opens its pincers. They scare the danger away. An earwig eats old leaves and fruit.

WOODLOUSE
about 15 millimetres long

A woodlouse is grey. It likes to live in a dark place, like Little Miss Tiny's mousehole. It comes out at night to feed, when it is cool and damp. A woodlouse eats dead wood and old leaves. It is a shy creature, and runs away when Little Miss Tiny goes near it. It curls up into a tight ball if Little Miss Tiny tries to pick it up.

about creepy-crawlies

LADYBIRD
about 5 millimetres long

A ladybird is a beetle. Little Miss Tiny is very happy to have one in her house. It eats the pests that harm her plants, such as greenflies. This ladybird has seven black spots on its red body. Others have two spots, or as many as twenty-two. Some ladybirds are black with red spots. Some are yellow with black spots.

HOUSE SPIDER
body about 15 millimetres long

Sometimes, when Little Miss Tiny is sitting very still, she sees a long-legged spider racing across her carpet! It stops when it reaches the skirting board – and that's when Little Miss Tiny counts its eight hairy legs. No wonder it can run so fast!

How many spots can you count on a ladybird?

Mr Snow's ice-cream pudding

YOU WILL NEED

a large tub of soft vanilla ice-cream

2 teaspoons of cinnamon powder

a few raisins, sultanas, glacé cherries, dried apricots, crystallised ginger, candied peel, chocolate buttons, chocolate raisins

a large mixing bowl

a plastic pudding basin

tin foil

1 Put the ice-cream into the mixing bowl.

2 Add the fruit, ginger, peel and chocolate. Mix together well. Stir in the cinnamon powder.

3 Put the mixture into the pudding basin. Cover with foil. Place in the freezer. Leave for about two hours – be patient!

4 To serve, turn the ice-cream pudding onto a plate.

I like to eat this pudding on a hot summer's day.

Laugh with Mr Cheerful

Mr Noisy, what did the shoe say to the foot?

I don't know, tell me.

You're having me on!

Mr Brave, why didn't the skeleton go to the disco?

I don't know, tell me.

It had no body to go with!

Mr Jelly, what wobbles when it flies?

I don't know, tell me.

A jellycopter!

Mr Sneeze, what's hairy and coughs?

I don't know, tell me.

A coconut with a cold!

Mr Rush in Sleepyland

One day,  sent a . It said: "Please come to my for a surprise." lived in Sleepyland, and had never been there before. He packed **1** big red , and **2** small blue . Then he put on his yellow and set off to 's . On the way he ran past a , a , and , who called out: "What's the hurry ? Where are you going to?" didn't stop. He just kept on running, faster than a or an , faster than a , or a . When he reached Sleepyland, a said: "Slow down, please." Then a said: "Please don't run!"

[image: Mr. Nosey] looked around Sleepyland. It was a very sleepy place. He saw a [cloud] fast asleep at the top of a [tree]. Then he saw a [kite] lying on the [grass] – it was too sleepy to fly. In Sleepyland the [flowers] are so sleepy they bend their heads over and go to sleep. [Mr. Rush] knocked on [Mr. Lazy]'s [door]. He lived in Yawn Cottage. There was no reply. "I bet he's fast asleep in his [bed]," said [Mr. Rush]. All the running around had made him feel very hungry. Off he went to buy some [sandwiches] and [bananas]. But the [shops] were closed – all except one. Only the [bed] shop was open. [Mr. Rush] could hear someone snoring inside. It was [Mr. Lazy], fast asleep on the biggest [bed]! [Mr. Rush] tickled him with a [feather]. But [Mr. Lazy] didn't wake up – what a surprise! "Time to go," said [Mr. Rush]. "Bye!"

mr. Nosey

mr. Rush

Mr Sneeze in Coldland

Mr Sneeze lives in a far away country called Coldland. It's so cold that people who live there don't need fridges or freezers in which to keep their food. They can leave ice-creams, and ice-lollies, and ice-cubes on their kitchen tables all day long, and they won't melt.

Mr Sneeze's cottage is in a town called Shivertown. It's a pretty little cottage which is always covered in snow.

Every morning, Mr Sneeze looks out of his bedroom window, and every morning the same thing happens. He sneezes... not once... not twice... but three times, very quickly, one after the other.

His first sneeze is quite small: "Atishoo." His second sneeze is louder: "Atish-OO." His third sneeze is the loudest of all: "A-TISH-OO!", at which point the cottage shivers and shudders, and all the snow slides off the roof and lands in the garden. It makes a loud thudding noise as it hits the ground. THUD!

Mr Sneeze's garden isn't a garden with green grass, or red

ATISHOO!

flowers, or brown trees. It's a snow garden with white snowmen, which Mr Sneeze is very good at making, white snowdrops, white snowdrifts and lots of white snowballs.

Well, one morning, after he'd sneezed the snow off the roof, he went into his snow garden. And do you know what he saw? First, he saw something orange and twisty coming out from underneath the fallen snow. It looked like it might be someone's long bendy arm. Then he saw something pink and round bulging up through the snow. It looked like it might be someone's big round tummy.

Mr Sneeze felt like he was going to sneeze again. It felt like it was going to be a much bigger sneeze than before.

"A-TISH-OOO!" sneezed Mr Sneeze. This sneeze was so big that it blew all the snow off the ground and back up onto the roof of his cottage. THUD!

And who do you think he found lying under the snow? The long bendy arm belonged to Mr Tickle, and the big round tummy belonged to Mr Greedy.

What a surprise they got when all the snow slithered off the roof of Mr Sneeze's cottage. It had covered them from top to toe. And now they were so cold their feet felt like blocks of ice, and their noses were starting to itch.

"Oh dear," said Mr Tickle. "I think we're catching Coldland colds."

"And I'm starting to feel hungry," said Mr Greedy, who was patting his big empty tummy.

"You can have a plate of frozen peas and a glass of orange iceade," said Mr Sneeze. "Or a freezing fishcake and an ice-cube to suck."

"YUCK!" said Mr Greedy, who didn't like the sound of that.

Just then, Mr Sneeze started to scrunch up his eyes. His mouth started to open... wide, then wider still. His nose began to twitch, and his head began to shake a little.

"Oh no!" called out Mr Tickle. "He's going to sneeze again!"

"A-TISH-OOO-OOO!" sneezed Mr Sneeze, even louder and longer than before.

Mr Tickle looked up at the snow on the roof of the cottage. It was still there. It hadn't moved. Not so much as one teeny, weeny little flake of snow had fallen down this time.

"Phew!" said Mr Tickle, holding up his long bendy arms, ready to catch any snow that did fall.

Mr Greedy didn't say anything. But his big, round, empty, hungry tummy did. First it said: "Blu-rrp," followed by: "GRR-UMPH," and then, just in case no one had heard it the first time: "BLU-RRP!"

That did it. The last noisy tummy rumble was enough to shake the snow on the roof … and down it started to slide, past the chimney, over the roof tiles, past Mr Sneeze's bedroom window, and into the snow garden below. THUD!

Mr Tickle and Mr Greedy didn't wait for the snow to hit the ground. They ran, and skated, and slid away as fast as they could, back to somewhere warm.

As for Mr Sneeze, well, he'd still got the whole of the day to make more snowmen for his snow garden! What a lovely start to his day.

Mr Muddle's ships and boats

Poor old Mr Muddle, he never does anything right. He gets everything the wrong way round. He puts his coat on backwards, and his gloves on inside out. He even walks backwards, which is a very muddled-up thing to do. He lives near Seatown, and he likes to watch the ships and boats coming and going. Here are some photographs he's taken... but he seems to have got the names mixed up. Can you help him?

IS IT A CANOE OR A CRUISE LINER?

OCEANIC INDEPENDENCE

This ship takes passengers across the sea. Mr Muddle went on one, but he should have been on an aeroplane instead!

Can you tell which is which for me?

IS IT A YACHT OR A CANOE?

IS IT A YACHT OR A TANKER?

This boat has a sail. It is blown along by the wind. Mr Muddle watches it sailing around Seatown's bay.

Mr Muddle has paddled along in one of these. He got very wet. It's not very big, and it doesn't go fast. There are lots in Seatown.

IS IT A TANKER OR A CRUISE LINER?

This ship is very long. It sails around the world, carrying oil inside it. It is far too big to sail into Seatown's little harbour.

Little Miss Shy plays

1 Little Miss Shy lives all alone in a little house called Thimble Cottage. It's tucked away out of sight, down a windy lane and across the fields.

2 Thimble Cottage is very, very hard to find, which is exactly the way Little Miss Shy likes it. The postman forgets the way there sometimes.

3 One day there was a knock at her door. Little Miss Shy hid behind an armchair. She was too shy to open the door. She blushed as red as a tomato.

4 Then there was a tapping noise on her window. She hid under a table, and put her hands over her ears. "Please go away," she whispered.

5 But out of the corner of one eye she saw the letterbox open, and a little pink foot poked through it. Someone was climbing into her house!

6 Little Miss Shy ran into her bedroom. And jumped onto her bed. And pulled the sheets over her. And the curtains. And the carpet too!

hide and seek

7 The stairs in Thimble Cottage were very old and creaky. Little Miss Shy could hear the sound of footsteps coming up the creaky old staircase.

8 She heard her bedroom door open. She heard someone walk around the bed. She felt someone tug the sheets. And the curtains. And the carpet!

9 Little Miss Shy kept very still. She blushed from head to toe. As red as a field of poppies. As red as a ladybird. "I feel very hot," she said, quietly.

10 So she popped one foot over the edge of the bed. Then the other. "There, I feel cooler now," she said. But then someone tickled her feet!

11 Little Miss Shy began to laugh. And as she laughed she wriggled, and fell out of bed. BUMP! Then she saw Little Miss Tiny holding a feather.

12 "That was a good game of hide and seek," said Little Miss Tiny. "Let's play again!" And then, Little Miss Shy didn't feel quite so shy after all!

Mr Tall's

MOUNT EVEREST
a mountain in Nepal

Mr Tall has found out that Mount Everest is the tallest mountain in the world. It's covered in snow and ice all the year round. Long-haired yaks live at the bottom of the mountain. People use them to carry heavy packages.

Mr Tall keeps a notebook. It's a very tall notebook. You can see some of its pages here. Whenever he finds out something interesting about a tall building, a tall animal, or a tall plant, he draws a picture and writes about it in his notebook. Today he's been finding out about tall mountains.

MOUNT FUJI
a mountain in Japan

This snow-covered mountain is an old volcano. It's the tallest mountain in Japan. Mr Tall has found out that people climb to the top each summer, to watch the sun rise in the morning.

TALL MOUNTAINS

MAUNA KEA
a mountain in Hawaii

This mountain is really a volcano. Most of it is under the sea. Only the top pokes up above the water level. Mr Tall has found out that if this underwater mountain was on dry land, then it would be even taller than Mount Everest.

BEN NEVIS
a mountain in Scotland

This is the tallest mountain in the United Kingdom. Mr Tall has worked out that you would have to stand six Ben Nevises on top of each other to reach the top of Mount Everest!

Have you ever climbed a mountain or a hill?

© Telegraph Colour Library

41

Little Miss Contrary in Muddleland

Muddleland is a very mixed-up place. Or as they say in Muddleland, it's a very muxed-ip place.

For instance, in Muddleland worms live in trees, and birds live in holes in the ground. For example, cars fly in the sky, and aeroplanes drive along the roads. As for the people who live in Muddleland, well, they never know if they are coming and going, or going and coming.

Little Miss Contrary lives in Muddleland. She would, wouldn't she? If you ask her to sing a song, she stands on her head. And if you ask her to count to ten, she tells you the time instead. You see, Little Miss Contrary always does the opposite of what you expect her to do.

One day, Little Miss Contrary had a cold. "Oh good, a warm!" she said.

What she meant to say was: "Oh no, a cold," but, of course, it didn't come out like that.

She started to look for her

42

tissues. She found them in a cornflake box. And guess what she found in the tissue box. Cornflakes. Lots of old, soggy cornflakes.

She poured milk on the tissues… and blew her nose on the cornflakes! What a muddle she was in.

She turned on the radio. And tried to put a slice of bread into it. She thought it was the toaster!

"It's going to be a wet and windy day," said the weatherman on the radio.

Umbrellas were flapping inside out.

She put on a pair of sunglasses and went into her garden… and was blown off her feet by a big gust of wind. She landed in a tree. Next to a worm, of course.

The next gust of wind blew her on to the roof of her house… and straight down her chimney!

She was covered from head to toe in black soot.

"I'm having a very good day!" she said, but what

she should have said was "I'm not having a very good day!"

She decided to have a bath, to wash the soot off. But instead she climbed into bed. And fell fast asleep, which was probably the best place for her! Wasn't it?

"A warm and sunny day!" repeated Little Miss Contrary, saying exactly the opposite.

She looked out of her window. Leaves were blowing off the trees.

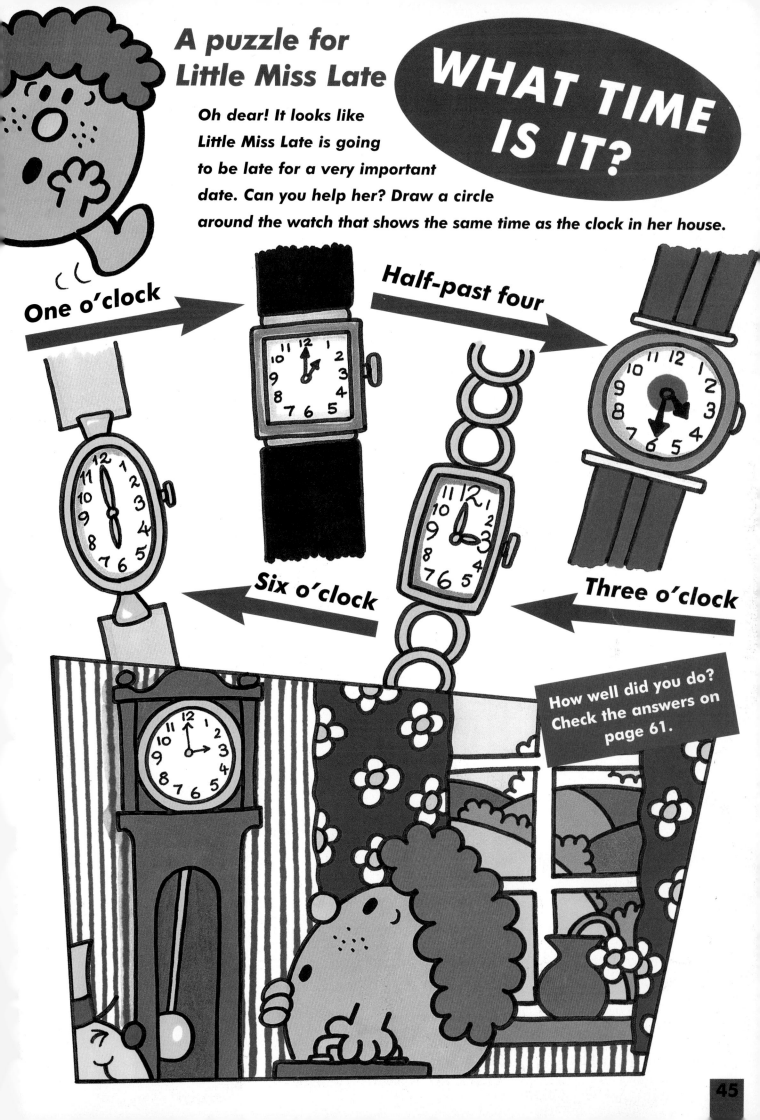

Little Miss Greedy's crunchy log

1 Put the cream, cocoa powder and icing sugar into the mixing bowl.

2 Whisk together until the mixture goes stiff. This might take a few minutes. Don't give up!

3 Spread some of the mixture onto a biscuit. Stick another biscuit to it. Keep doing this until you have joined all the biscuits together. Only use about half the mixture.

4 Spread the rest of the mixture over the outside of the biscuits. Cover them as much as possible. Make a bark pattern by dragging a fork through the cream.

I like to eat this pudding on a hot summer's day.

5 Put the log in the fridge. Leave for about thirty minutes before serving. Sift a little icing sugar over it so it looks like snow. Add some cherries if you want to.

Little Miss Scatterbrain's wild flowers

Little Miss Scatterbrain lives in Buttercup Cottage in the middle of a wood. It's a very pretty cottage with lots of wild flowers in the garden. The only trouble is, Little Miss Scatterbrain keeps on forgetting their names. She even forgets the name of her cottage sometimes, and calls it Daisy Cottage, or Tulip Cottage, or even Hyacinth Cottage. Here are some of the pretty flowers she sees around her cottage and in the wood nearby.

SNOWDROP
flowers from January to March

When all the garden is covered in snow, Little Miss Scatterbrain looks for the drooping, bell-shaped snowdrop flowers. They are a sign that the warmer days of spring are coming.

PRIMROSE
flowers from January to May

Primroses bring colour to Little Miss Scatterbrain's garden during the long dark months of winter. Most are yellow, but some are purple.

Please don't pick wild flowers. Leave them for other people to enjoy too. Thank you.

BLUEBELL
flowers from April to June

Little Miss Scatterbrain likes to walk in the wood when the bluebells are in flower. There are so many they cover the ground like a big blue blanket.

Which wild flowers have you seen?

POPPY
flowers from June to August

Red poppies and yellow poppies grow in Little Miss Scatterbrain's garden. When the flowers have died she shakes the seed pods, scattering seeds which will grow into new plants next year.

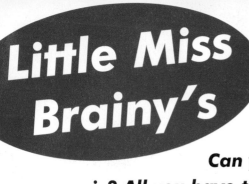

Little Miss Brainy's home from home quiz

Can you do Little Miss Brainy's quiz? All you have to do is decide if each sentence is true or false. The first one has been done for you.

1 Mr Nosey lives in Muddleland

TRUE ☐   FALSE ☑

2 Mr Sneeze lives in Coldland

TRUE ☐   FALSE ☑

3 Mr Lazy lives in Sleepyland

TRUE ☐   FALSE ☐

4 Mr Nonsense lives in Loudland

TRUE ☑   FALSE ☐

5 Mr Happy lives in Cleverland

TRUE ☑   FALSE ☐

6 Little Miss Twins live in Threeland

TRUE ☑   FALSE ☐

The answers are on page 61

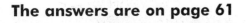

Mr Small's round the bend maze

Mr Small has been walking in circles for ages! He's stuck inside this round maze, and can't see over the hedge to find his way out. Can you show him the way?

NO EXIT!

NOT HERE

EXIT!

KEEP GOING!

51

Mr Dizzy in Cleverland

Cleverland is the place where clever people live. And clever worms. And clever pigs. And even clever elephants. They spend their time asking each other really tricky questions, such as: 'What is the opposite of black?' and: 'What's big and grey and has big ears and a trunk?' If you can answer these questions, then you could live in Cleverland too.

Now, it so happens that there is one person who lives in Cleverland who is not quite so clever. It's Mr Dizzy. He thinks orange is the opposite of black! And he thinks a big grey animal with a trunk is a mouse!

It's no use asking why Mr Dizzy lives in Cleverland. He just does. He lives in a rather dizzy house, which he built himself. It's on the side of a hill. It looks as though it might slide down the hill at any moment. If his house had a name it would be called

Crooked Cottage, or Wonky Cottage, or Tipsy Cottage.

For instance, the front door leans so much that Mr Dizzy has to lean right over to go through it. And if he leans over too much… he falls flat on his face!

For example, when Mr Dizzy turns the taps on in his bath, the water fills up at one end only and then pours out over the edge. It goes straight through the ceiling… and into the kitchen sink, which is where he ends up having his bath!

One day Mr Dizzy decided to go for a walk. Before he set off he looked out of his bedroom window, to see what the weather was doing. "Looks like it might rain. Must remember to take my umbrella," he said. But by the time he got downstairs he'd forgotten what he'd just said – so he went walking without his umbrella. And his raincoat. And his wellington boots.

Just as Mr Dizzy reached the bottom of the hill it began to rain. Only in Cleverland the rain doesn't fall in tiny drops, or little spots, or teeny splashes. In Cleverland the rain falls in great big drops as big as puddles. Which meant, of course, that Mr Dizzy got rather wet.

Everyone else put up their umbrellas, and put on their raincoats and wellington boots.

They didn't get wet at all. How very clever of them.

But as for Mr Dizzy, he held out his arms and jumped into as many puddles as he could find. Did he mind getting so wet? Not at all! "This is the best bath I've had all week!" he said.

After the rain stopped he saw a notice on a tree. It said:

CLEVER QUIZ TODAY

answer a question and win a prize

"That sounds easy," said Mr Dizzy. Off he went to the quiz.

But it wasn't as easy as Mr Dizzy had expected. Little Miss Brainy was in charge of the quiz.

First of all she asked Mr Sneeze, "What's the capital of Coldland?"

"Shivertown!" said Mr Sneeze. "It's where I live!" Little Miss Brainy gave him a huge box of tissues as his prize.

Then she asked Little Miss Lucky, "Who lives in Horseshoe Cottage?"

"I do!" said Little Miss Lucky. Her prize was a shiny new horseshoe to put on her door.

Then it was Mr Dizzy's turn. "What jam can't you put on your bread?" asked Little Miss Brainy.

"Erm," said Mr Dizzy.

"Hurry up," said Little Miss Brainy.

"Can I have a clue please?" asked Mr Dizzy. "It's a really difficult question."

Just at that moment everyone heard a car horn. PEEP! PEEP! it went. And again. And again.

It was Mr Funny who was sitting in his car. He was stuck behind Mr Strong in his car, who was stuck behind Little Miss Splendid in her car. They were all coming to the quiz.

Suddenly Mr Dizzy remembered Little Miss Brainy's question. "I know the answer!" he shouted. "It was a trick question. You can't put traffic jam on your bread!" Which,

of course, was the right answer.

Guess what Little Miss Brainy gave Mr Dizzy for his prize. It was a certificate. It said:

Mr Dizzy
Cleverest person I know

But you know, don't you, that if she'd asked him what the opposite of black was, he'd have said orange... or blue... or green!

PEEP! PEEP!

Little Miss Magic's

Little Miss Magic lives in Abracadabra Cottage.
Every day she practises her best magic tricks. She likes to make things disappear. Can you spot five things she has made disappear from the bottom picture?

Check your answers on page 61

Make a flag with Mr Tickle

On pages 22 and 23 are some flags drawn by Mr Tickle for six of his friends. Here's how you can make your own flag for one of your favourite Mr Men and Little Miss friends.

Little Miss Sunshine

Mr. Small

Little Miss Dotty

Mr. Tall

1 Cut out a rectangle from the white paper. It should measure about 20cm wide and 15cm high.

2 Decide which of your Mr Men or Little Miss friends you are going to make the flag for. Draw a design in pencil on one side of the paper. You can see some ideas on the side of this page.

3 Colour in your design. Wait for it to dry if you have used paints.

Now you can fly your flag with me!

4 Use sticky tape to fasten the straw to the back of the flag.

Mr Bump's bumpy foggy day

1 Mr Bump was in a hurry to get to the post office with a letter. But when he opened his front door, he saw that everywhere was covered in fog.

2 He couldn't see further than the end of his nose, which for Mr Bump isn't very far at all. "I do hope I don't bump into anything," he said.

3 He put his hands in front of him and began to walk slowly along the footpath. He touched a tree, and carefully walked around it. But then…

4 "Ouch!" said a little voice. "You're standing on my head!" It was Mr Small. "Sorry," said Mr Bump. "I didn't see you because of all the fog."

5 He carried on walking… and bumped into something big and round and soft. It made a grumbly noise. "Mind my tummy," said Mr Greedy.

6 "I think I'll sit down and wait for the fog to clear," said Mr Bump. But he sat on Mr Lazy who was having a nap. "Get off me!" growled Mr Lazy.

7 Then Mr Bump tripped over Mr Tall's left foot. He went head over heels, clonked his chin, banged his knee, knocked his nose, and rolled down a hill.

8 "Help!" cried out Mr Bump. "I can't stop!" He rolled so far that he went straight past the post office, and past the postman on his bike.

9 He only came to a stop when he bumped into Mr Funny's car which was parked at the side of the road. "Can't drive in this fog," said Mr Funny.

10 "I have to post my letter," said Mr Bump. "And now I'm a long way from the post office." "There's a pillar box by that tree," said Mr Funny.

11 Mr Bump went as carefully as he could to the pillar box. He popped his letter inside, and then went back to Mr Funny, without falling over once.

12 "Who's the letter for?" asked Mr Funny. "Oh silly me!" said Mr Bump. "It's for you!" And he laughed and bumped the car horn. PEEP! PEEP!

Join Our Club!

MR. MEN & little miss CLUB

When you become a member of the fantastic Mr Men and Little Miss Club you'll receive a personal letter from Mr Happy and Little Miss Giggles, a club badge with your name on it, and a superb Welcome Pack that will delight you.

You'll also get birthday and Christmas cards from the Mr Men and Little Misses, a regular newsletter crammed with special offers, privileges and news, and a Mr Men catalogue including great party ideas.

If it were on sale in the shops, the Welcome Pack alone would cost around £12.00. But a year's membership is just £9.99 (plus 73p postage) with a 14 day money-back guarantee if you are not delighted.

Membership card ✓ Personalised badge ✓ Exclusive Club cassette with Mr Men stories and songs ✓ Mr Men keyring ✓ Mr Men sticker book ✓ Tiny Mr Men floc model ✓ Club pencil ✓ Personal Mr Men notebook ✓ Mr Men bendy pen ✓ Mr eraser ✓ Mr Men book mark ✓ Mr Men diary ✓ Copy of Mr Men magazine ✓

Save £2 on the Club T-Shirt!
Order this fantastic Club T-Shirt when you join the Club and you can get it for just £3.99 instead of the usual £5.99. Available in ages 3-4, 5-6 and 7-8.

To be completed by an adult

Please enrol the following in Mr Men & Little Miss Club at £10.72 (inc postage).

Member's Full Name : _____ Address:_____

_____ Post Code:_____ Date of birth:____/____/____

Your Name:_____ Address (if different):_____

_____ Post Code:_____

Name of child's parent or guardian (if not you):_____

Please also send me a Club T-Shirt at £3.99. Tick size ___ age 3-4 ___ age 5-6 ___ age 7-8.

Total amount due: £_____ (£10.72 per membership, £3.99 per T-Shirt)

❏ I enclose a cheque or postal order payable to Mr Men & Little Miss Club

❏ Please charge my MasterCard (Access) / Visa account.

Card number: ☐☐☐☐ ☐☐☐☐ ☐☐☐☐ ☐☐☐☐ ☐☐☐☐ Expiry Date: _____/_____

Data Protection Act: If you do **not** wish to receive other family offers from us or companies we recommend, please tick this box ❏

WI

A Robell Club

How to Enrol
Return the coupon to: Mr Men & Little Miss Happy Land, PO Box 142, Horsham RH13 Credit card orders may call 01403 2427 or fax 01403 261555

Allow 28 days for delivery. Promoter: Robell Me Promotions Limited. The money-back guarantee do affect your statutory rights. Birthday and Christmas are sent care of parent/guardians in advance of th

MR MEN & LITTLE MISS ™ & 1998 Mrs Roger Hargreave

Answers

pages 16 and 17
Mr Clever helps Mr Dizzy

1 Worm number 4 is the odd one out because he is not wearing glasses.
2 Bird number 1 is the odd one out because he is flying the other way.
3 Plate number 1 has five sweets on it.
4 Flower number 2 has six petals.
5 Mr Small is holding balloon number 3.

page 20
Little Miss Greedy's spot the difference

1 The cherries are missing from one cake.
2 A cake is missing from the plate.
3 Mr Funny is missing.
4 The window is missing from the door of Cherrycake Cottage.
5 Little Miss Greedy's tongue is missing.

pages 22 and 23
Fly the flag with Mr Tickle

1 The flag with the cake belongs to Mr Greedy.
2 The flag with the question mark belongs to Little Miss Curious.
3 The flag with the plaster belongs to Mr Bump.
4 The flag with the wand belongs to Little Miss Magic.
5 The flag with the bag belongs to Little Miss Tidy.
6 The flag with the drum belongs to Mr Noisy.

page 44
Who lives where?

Mr Happy lives in Happyland.
Mr Nosey lives in Tiddletown.
Mr Quiet lives in Loudland.
Mr Sneeze lives in Coldland.

page 45
What time is it?

The clock in Little Miss Late's house says **three o'clock.**

page 50
Little Miss Brainy's home from home quiz

1 False. Mr Nosey lives in Tiddletown.
2 True.
3 True.
4 False. Mr Nonsense lives in Nonsenseland.
5 False. Mr Happy lives in Happyland.
6 False. Little Miss Twins live in Twoland.

page 56
Little Miss Magic's spot the difference

1 Two cushion tassels are missing.
2 A cup and saucer are missing.
3 A flower from the vase is missing.
4 The picture in the frame is missing.
5 The pattern on the vase is missing.